THE ROMAN PROVINCE OF DACIA, SEPTEMBER, A.D. 117

HHHH...
HHHH...
HHHH...

HK... AGH!
OH, GODS...
SPARE ME--
NO.

NOT YET.

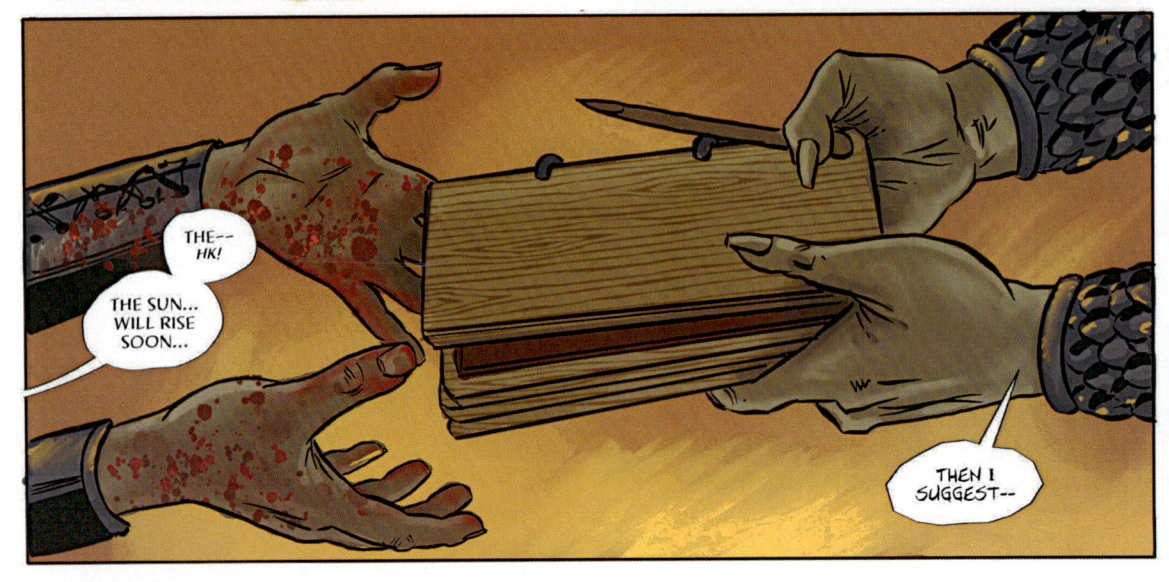

"-- THAT YOU WRITE QUICKLY."
THE ROMAN PROVINCE OF SYRIA, OCTOBER, A.D. 117.
KNOCK KNOCK
ENTER.
DISPATCHES FROM DACIA HAVE ARRIVED, CAESAR.
FROM TIBERIUS CLAUDIUS MAXIMUS.
CLAUDIUS?
WE'VE HEARD NOTHING FROM HIM IN MONTHS.
FIVE MONTHS, TO BE PRECISE, CAESAR...
...DO EITHER OF YOU SMELL SOME-THING...?
HE'S SENT A LARGE PACKET.
THERE'S THIS--
--AND THIS.
UGH!
BY THE GODS, WHAT IS THAT SMELL?
THE PACKET SPENT SOME TIME IN TRANSIT, CAESAR. PART OF THAT ON A FISHING BOAT. I WAS TOLD THE NOTEBOOK IS THE PRIORITY.
PUT THE BAG IN THE CORNER--THE FAR ONE--AND LEAVE US.
AND GO TAKE A BATH!

THERE WAS NO HINT OF THIS DARKNESS ON THE LONG-AGO DAY THAT YOUR LATE FATHER, THE DIVINE TRAJAN, LED THE LEGIONS ACROSS THE ISTER INTO DACIA.
ONLY THE RENEWED PROMISE OF CONQUEST, GLORY, AND EMPIRE WITHOUT END.
YET DARKNESS LAY IN WAIT FOR US, SHADOWING US FROM THE MINUTE WE CROSSED APOLLODORUS'S INVASION BRIDGE.
WE FELT UNSTOPPABLE. THE DACIAN ARMIES COULD NOT WITHSTAND US, THEIR GOLD POURED INTO OUR COFFERS, AND THEIR PEOPLE FELL LIKE HAY BEFORE OUR SWEEPING SCYTHE.
THE DARKNESS WAITED EAGERLY AS WE TORE DOWN THE WALLS THAT KEPT IT FROM US.
THAT OLD WOLF KING DECEBALUS COULD ONLY CUT HIS OWN THROAT WHEN HE SAW US COMING FOR HIM.
WE THOUGHT THAT WAS THE END OF IT, THE WAR OVER AND WON.
BUT THAT WAS THE MOMENT WE LOST.

I KNOW THIS IS A VERY DIFFERENT SENTIMENT FROM MY LAST REPORT, ALL THOSE MONTHS AGO.
BUT THE VAGUE REPORTS OF "UNREST," "ATTACKS" AND "REVOLT" PROMPTING YOU TO SEND ME BACK SEEMED LUDICROUS WHEN I FIRST ARRIVED.
LETHARGY AND TIMIDITY WERE WIDESPREAD. PEOPLE SCURRIED FROM DOORWAY TO DOORWAY AS IF THE SHADES OF DIS STALKED THEM.
TO SEE ROMANS BEHAVING THIS WAY, LIKE FRIGHTENED MICE, GOT DEEP UNDER MY SKIN.
I LOST MY TEMPER WITH A GUARDSMAN, A PATHETIC MAN WHO WHIMPERED AND CLUTCHED AT AN AMULET AROUND HIS NECK. I PITY HIM NOW, KNOWING WHAT I DO, BUT GODS, HE DISGUSTED ME THEN.
TELL ME, DAMN IT!
WHAT'S HAPPENING HERE?
AGH!
I'M SORRY, I'M SORRY--
OH GODS, PROTECT ME--
I CAN'T, IT WILL KNOW, IT WILL FIND ME--
WHAT WILL KNOW?
THE FOG.
CAN'T YOU SEE IT?

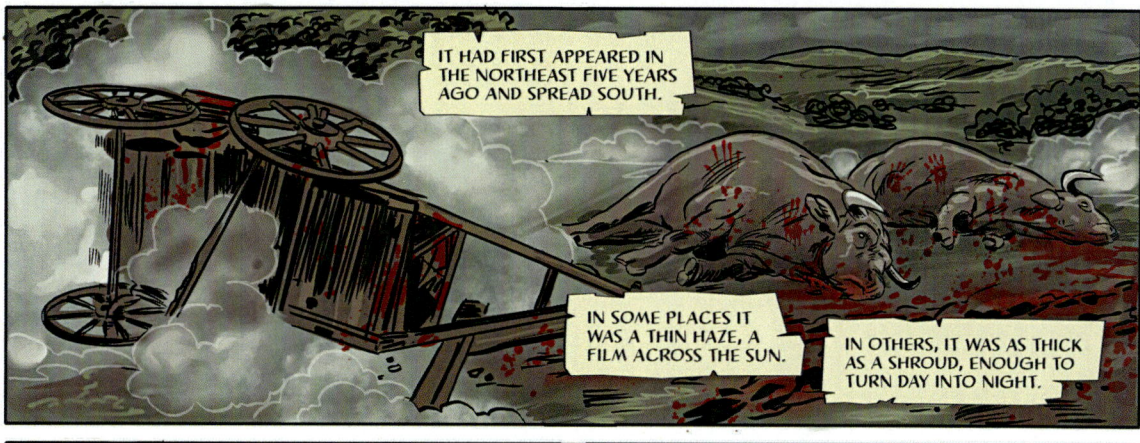

"THE FOG."

IT WAS SO STRANGE. I HAD SOMEHOW FAILED TO NOTICE IT BEFORE THIS WRETCH POINTED IT OUT.

BUT NOW I SAW IT EVERYWHERE.

IT HAD FIRST APPEARED IN THE NORTHEAST FIVE YEARS AGO AND SPREAD SOUTH.

IN SOME PLACES IT WAS A THIN HAZE, A FILM ACROSS THE SUN.

IN OTHERS, IT WAS AS THICK AS A SHROUD, ENOUGH TO TURN DAY INTO NIGHT.

WHEREVER IT FELL THICK, PEOPLE BEGAN TO DISAPPEAR. ONLY A FEW AT FIRST. BUT THEN REPORTS CAME IN OF CAMPS BEING FOUND EMPTY, ENTIRE VILLAGES DESERTED.

PEOPLE CALLED IT EMPUSA, THE WITCH-FOG. TARTARUS. THE LAMIA. HALF-JOKING NICKNAMES TO COVER THEIR GROWING UNEASE.

THEN, A WEEK BEFORE I ARRIVED, THEY HAD LOST CONTACT WITH A COLONY ON THE EASTERN FRONTIER.

BASSUS, THE PROVINCIAL GOVERNOR, SENT A COHORT THERE TO INVESTIGATE.

THEY WERE NEVER SEEN AGAIN.

AND THE PROVINCE ERUPTED INTO PANIC.

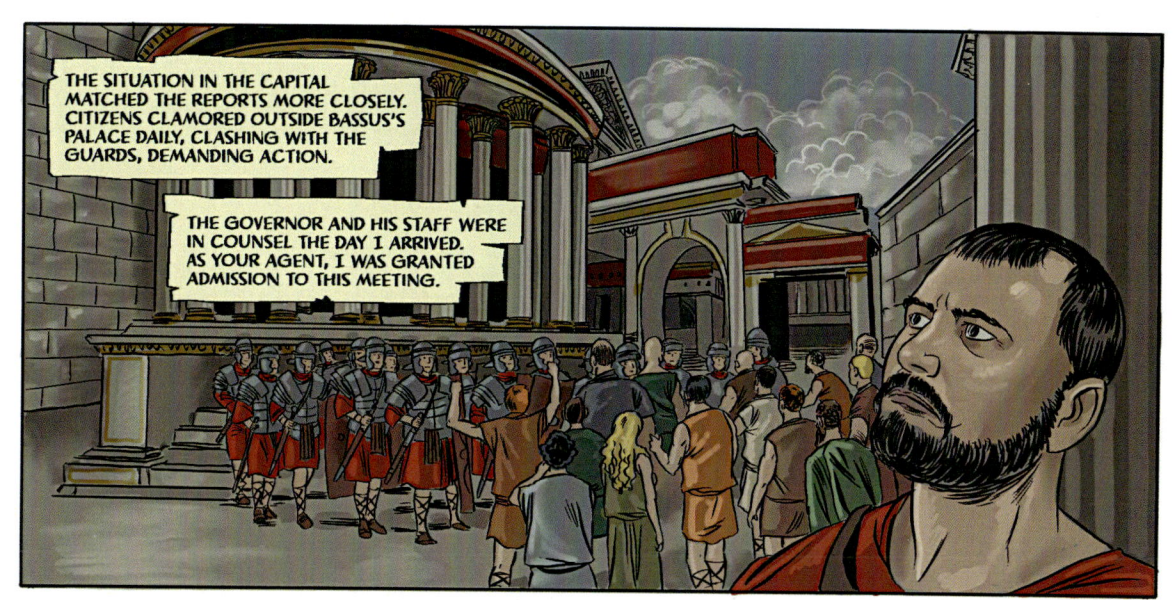

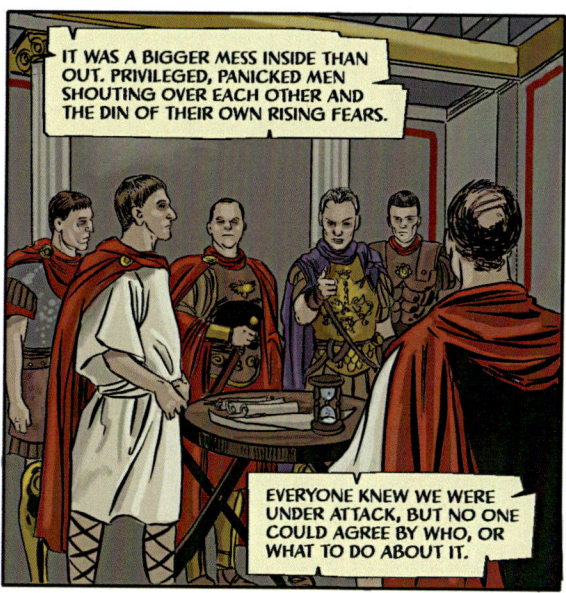

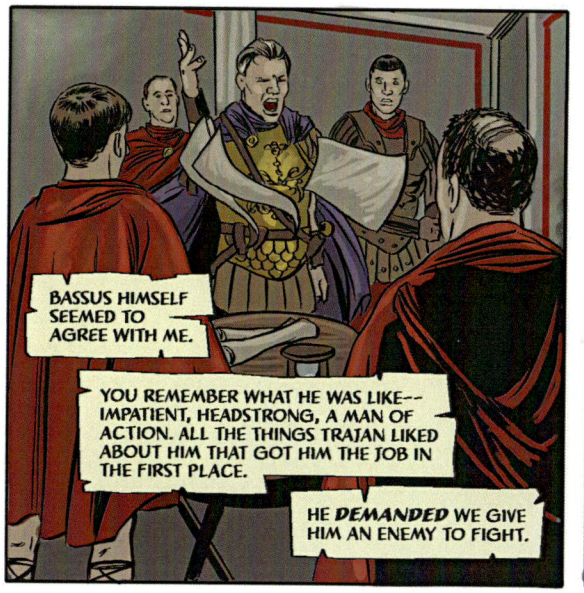

THE SITUATION IN THE CAPITAL MATCHED THE REPORTS MORE CLOSELY. CITIZENS CLAMORED OUTSIDE BASSUS'S PALACE DAILY, CLASHING WITH THE GUARDS, DEMANDING ACTION.

THE GOVERNOR AND HIS STAFF WERE IN COUNSEL THE DAY I ARRIVED. AS YOUR AGENT, I WAS GRANTED ADMISSION TO THIS MEETING.

IT WAS A BIGGER MESS INSIDE THAN OUT. PRIVILEGED, PANICKED MEN SHOUTING OVER EACH OTHER AND THE DIN OF THEIR OWN RISING FEARS.

EVERYONE KNEW WE WERE UNDER ATTACK, BUT NO ONE COULD AGREE BY WHO, OR WHAT TO DO ABOUT IT.

I AM ASHAMED TO SAY, CAESAR, THAT FOR THE SECOND TIME SINCE RETURNING, I FELT DISGUST FOR MY COUNTRYMEN.

THESE MEN WERE NOT THE GIANTS I HAD SERVED UNDER THE DIVINE TRAJAN. THEY WERE NOT THE CONQUERORS WHO TAMED THIS BARBARIAN LAND. THEY WERE PARALYZED AND INEFFECTIVE, MADE USELESS BY A DECADE OF PEACE.

BASSUS HIMSELF SEEMED TO AGREE WITH ME.

YOU REMEMBER WHAT HE WAS LIKE-- IMPATIENT, HEADSTRONG, A MAN OF ACTION. ALL THE THINGS TRAJAN LIKED ABOUT HIM THAT GOT HIM THE JOB IN THE FIRST PLACE.

HE **DEMANDED** WE GIVE HIM AN ENEMY TO FIGHT.

DAMN THESE FOG-BOUND IDIOTS, I THOUGHT.

AND I SET OUT TO FIND HIM ONE.

THEY WERE SO CONVINCED OF THEIR SPIRITS AND WITCH-FOG THAT THEY COULDN'T SEE THE FACTS IN FRONT OF THEM.
IN TEM
WHEN THEY WENT TO LOOK FOR THE MISSING COHORT, THEY HAD FOUND THE WHOLE COLONY NEARLY BURNT TO THE GROUND. WHOEVER DID THAT WANTED TO COVER THEIR TRACKS, SOMETHING SPIRITS DIDN'T CONCERN THEMSELVES WITH.
I WAS A TRACKER OF MEN ACROSS THREE DIFFERENT WARS, CAESAR.
I COULD TELL THAT, DESPITE THE COMPLETENESS OF THE DESTRUCTION, THE MEN WHO DID THIS HAD BEEN HURRIED. HURRIED MEN ARE DISTRACTED, AND WHEN THEY ARE DISTRACTED--
--THEY FORGET THINGS.

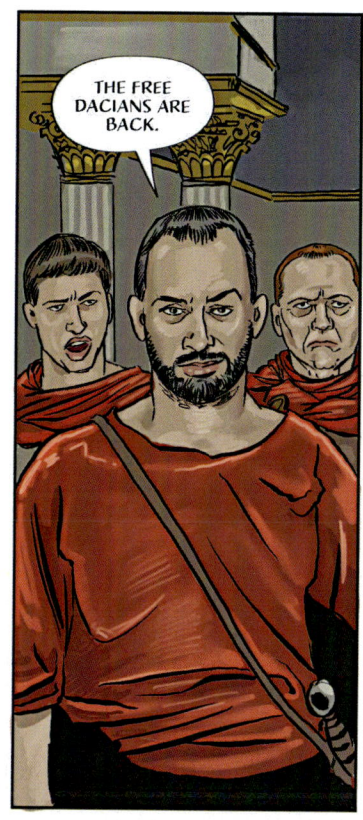

IT'S THE HEAD OF A CAVALRY STANDARD, GOVERNOR.

A *DACIAN* ONE.

CLNK

THE FREE DACIANS ARE BACK.

I SAW THE LIGHT BREAK THROUGH, AND THE CONFUSION LIFT FROM THEIR MINDS.

IT ALL FINALLY MADE SENSE.

THE FREE DACIANS WERE THE BARBARIAN REFUGEES WHO FLED NORTH OF THE KARPATES MOUNTAINS AT THE END OF THE WAR. THEY HAD FORMED A NEW NATION, WITH A NEW LEADER TO SUCCEED THE FALLEN DECEBALUS.

LITTLE WAS KNOWN ABOUT HIM. HE WAS RUMORED TO BE A PRINCE OF THE DACIAN ROYAL LINE WHO ESCAPED THE ROMAN PURGE. HIS IDENTITY AND RECORD DURING THE WAR WERE COMPLETE MYSTERIES TO THE ROMAN COMMAND, AS IF HE HAD NOT EVEN EXISTED UNTIL AFTER THE KINGDOM FELL.

HE WAS CALLED **BALAURUS**, AFTER A FEARSOME MONSTER OF DACIAN LEGEND.

AND HE WAS A MONSTER IN EVERY SENSE OF THE WORD.

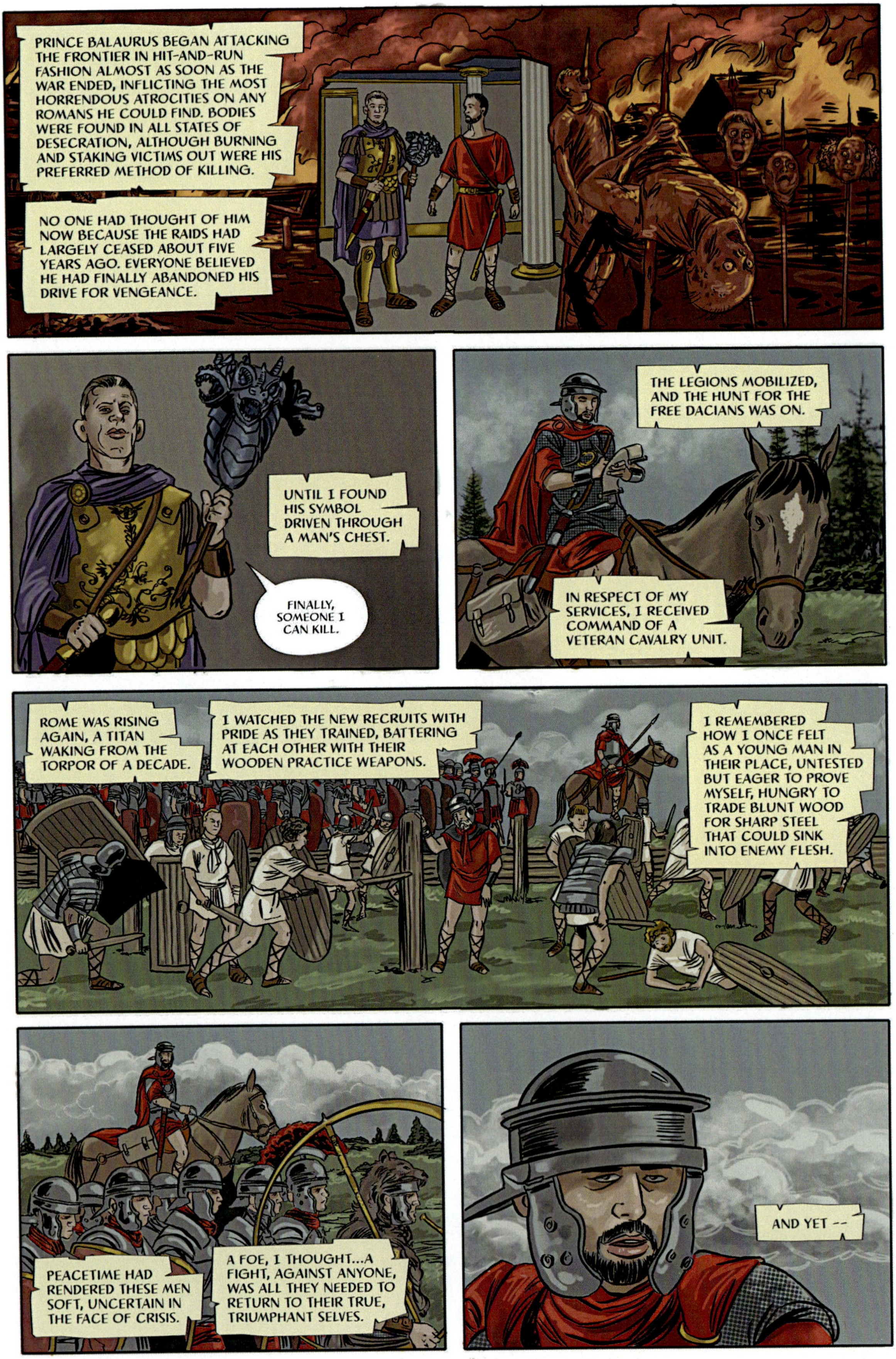
PRINCE BALAURUS BEGAN ATTACKING THE FRONTIER IN HIT-AND-RUN FASHION ALMOST AS SOON AS THE WAR ENDED, INFLICTING THE MOST HORRENDOUS ATROCITIES ON ANY ROMANS HE COULD FIND. BODIES WERE FOUND IN ALL STATES OF DESECRATION, ALTHOUGH BURNING AND STAKING VICTIMS OUT WERE HIS PREFERRED METHOD OF KILLING.
NO ONE HAD THOUGHT OF HIM NOW BECAUSE THE RAIDS HAD LARGELY CEASED ABOUT FIVE YEARS AGO. EVERYONE BELIEVED HE HAD FINALLY ABANDONED HIS DRIVE FOR VENGEANCE.
UNTIL I FOUND HIS SYMBOL DRIVEN THROUGH A MAN'S CHEST.
FINALLY, SOMEONE I CAN KILL.
THE LEGIONS MOBILIZED, AND THE HUNT FOR THE FREE DACIANS WAS ON.
IN RESPECT OF MY SERVICES, I RECEIVED COMMAND OF A VETERAN CAVALRY UNIT.
ROME WAS RISING AGAIN, A TITAN WAKING FROM THE TORPOR OF A DECADE.
I WATCHED THE NEW RECRUITS WITH PRIDE AS THEY TRAINED, BATTERING AT EACH OTHER WITH THEIR WOODEN PRACTICE WEAPONS.
I REMEMBERED HOW I ONCE FELT AS A YOUNG MAN IN THEIR PLACE, UNTESTED BUT EAGER TO PROVE MYSELF, HUNGRY TO TRADE BLUNT WOOD FOR SHARP STEEL THAT COULD SINK INTO ENEMY FLESH.
PEACETIME HAD RENDERED THESE MEN SOFT, UNCERTAIN IN THE FACE OF CRISIS.
A FOE, I THOUGHT...A FIGHT, AGAINST ANYONE, WAS ALL THEY NEEDED TO RETURN TO THEIR TRUE, TRIUMPHANT SELVES.
AND YET --

OUR PERFECT FOE DIDN'T SEEM TO UNDERSTAND HIS ROLE.

OUR SCOUTS AND SPIES FERRETED OUT THEIR HIDING PLACES. WE HOUNDED THEM EVERYWHERE, ATTACKING FEROCIOUSLY, KILLING DOZENS AT A TIME.

BUT THE MONSTERS WE SOUGHT WERE NEVER THERE. INSTEAD, THEY SEEMED DETERMINED, EVEN DESPERATE, TO TALK TO US, TO NEGOTIATE. A GROUP OF THEM TRIED TO *SURRENDER* ON THE CONDITION THAT WE LISTEN TO THEM. WE SLAUGHTERED THEM TO A MAN.

WE KILLED DACIANS BECAUSE WE NEEDED TO KILL *SOMETHING*. TO HIDE FROM THE FACT THAT WE WERE ACCOMPLISHING *NOTHING*.

BECAUSE IN SPITE OF IT ALL, ROMANS CONTINUED TO DIE, CONTINUED TO VANISH WITHOUT A TRACE, IN GREATER NUMBERS NOW THAN EVER BEFORE.

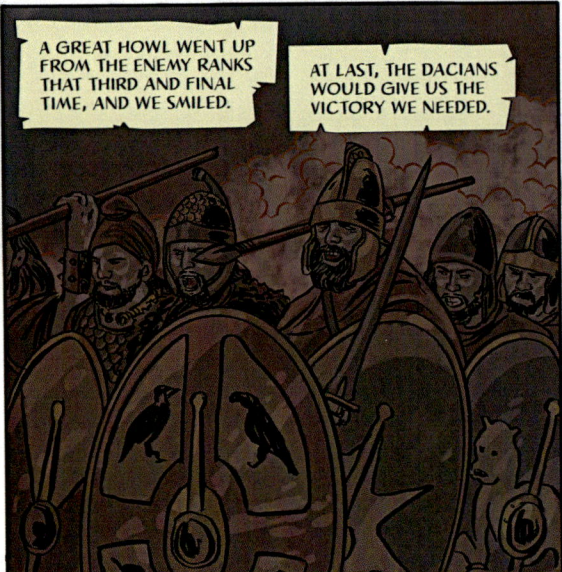

THEN CAME THE NEWS WE HAD BEEN PRAYING FOR...

...BALAURUS HIMSELF HAD BEEN FOUND, WITH HIS MAIN ARMY.

THEY WERE RACING TOWARD THE IRON GATE PASS, THE MAIN ARTERY INTO THE HEART OF THE PROVINCE.

BASSUS WAS THERE TO GREET THEM WHEN THEY ARRIVED.

MADDENINGLY, THEY TRIED TO PARLEY WITH US *AGAIN*. THREE SEPARATE TIMES THEY SENT THEIR HERALDS OVER TO OUR LINES. EACH TIME, WE SENT THEM BACK.

A GREAT HOWL WENT UP FROM THE ENEMY RANKS THAT THIRD AND FINAL TIME, AND WE SMILED.

AT LAST, THE DACIANS WOULD GIVE US THE VICTORY WE NEEDED.

SO EAGER WERE WE FOR BATTLE, THAT WE NEVER NOTICED THE *FOG* THAT HAD CREPT IN AMONG US.

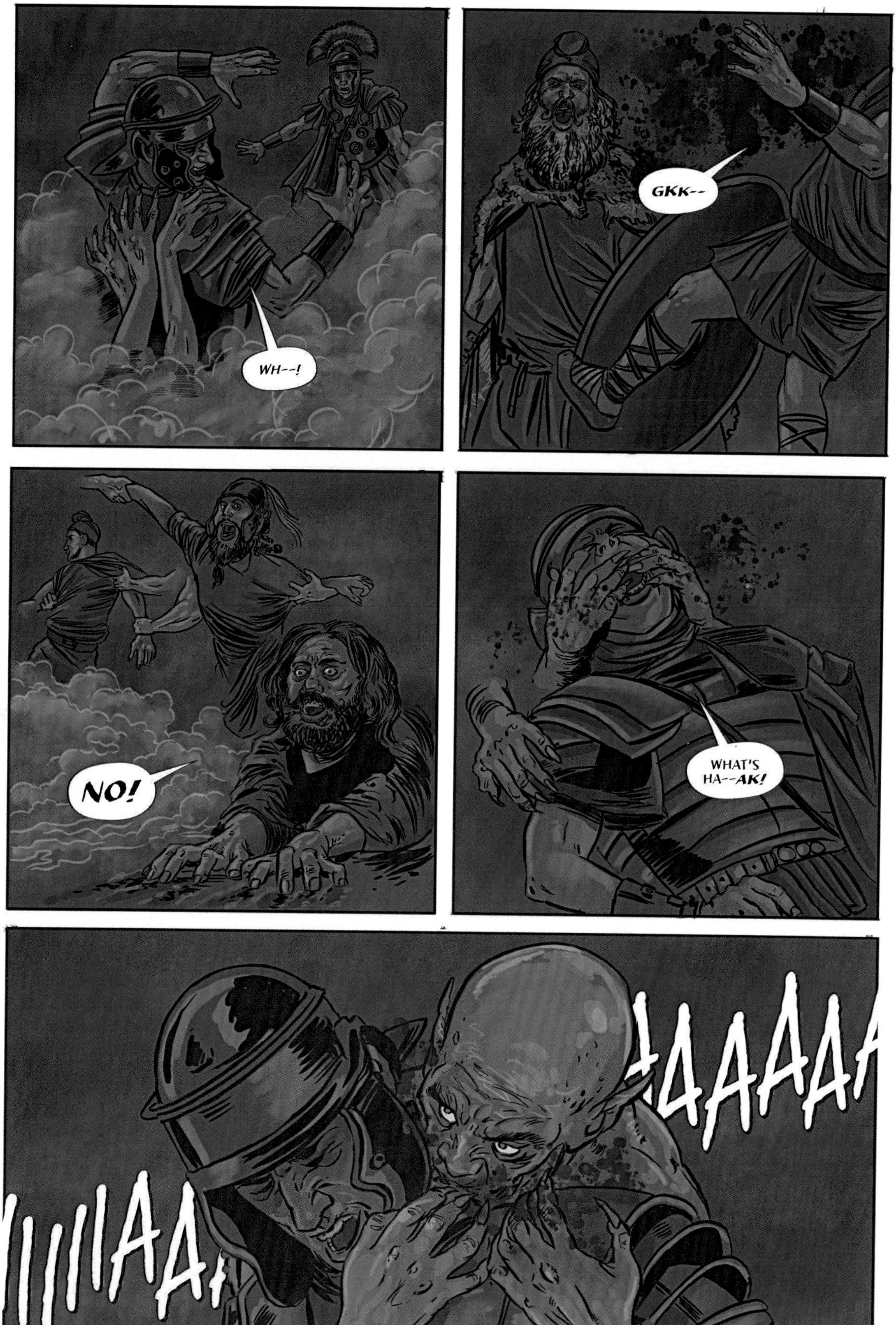
WH--!
GKK--
NO!
WHAT'S HA--AK!
AAAAAA
IIIIAA

AAAAAAAAAAAAAAA

AAAAAAAA

AAAAAAAAAAA

GAH!

THIS WAS THE ENEMY WE COULD NOT SEE, OF WHICH THE DACIANS HAD TRIED SO DESPERATELY TO WARN US.

THEY WERE UNLIKE ANYTHING I HAVE SEEN IN NATURE OR IN NIGHTMARE, RIPPING THROUGH BOTH OUR ARMIES LIKE WE WERE STRAW.

I WATCHED A SWARM OF THEM SWALLOW BASSUS WHOLE. I KNOW I WAS NOT THE ONLY WITNESS, FOR IT WAS AT THIS MOMENT--

--WE *ALL* BROKE AND RAN.

WE FLED TO THE ROMAN CAMP, FRIEND AND ENEMY TOGETHER, AND BARRICADED OURSELVES INSIDE THE STOCKADE, BARELY CONSIDERING WHAT POSSIBLE GOOD IT WOULD DO AGAINST THESE CREATURES.

WE COWERED THERE AS THEY RAGED OUTSIDE, HELPLESS, SCARED, WITH NO IDEA WHAT WAS HAPPENING OR WHY, JUST PRAYING TO THE GODS FOR A QUICK, MERCIFUL DEATH.

HEY!

THEY'VE STOPPED ATTACKING! THEY'RE JUST STANDING THERE!

WHY HAVEN'T THEY BROKEN THROUGH THE WALL?

IT SHOULD BE OBVIOUS.

THEY CAN'T.

THEY HAD US. THEY COULD HAVE RUSHED US AND KILLED US TO A MAN. IT WOULD HAVE BEEN OVER IN A MOMENT.

BUT THEY MADE NO MOVE TOWARD US.

DESPITE THEIR HATRED, WHICH WAS *PALPABLE*, IT WAS MORE IMPORTANT TO THEM NOW, AS IT HAD BEEN FROM THE BEGINNING, THAT THEY TALK TO US, AND WE LISTEN.

SO I PUSHED DOWN MY SCREAMING INSTINCTS--

--AND DEMANDED ANSWERS.

THEY CAN'T BREAK THROUGH A WALL OF *WOOD*?

THESE THINGS SHRUGGED OFF SWORD BLADES AND BALLISTA BOLTS. THEY LEAP THROUGH THE AIR LIKE LEOPARDS AND SHRED STEEL LIKE IT WAS *PARCHMENT*!

HOW CAN *YOU* POSSIBLY KNOW WHAT THEY CAN AND CANNOT DO?

BECAUSE THIS IS MY FAULT.

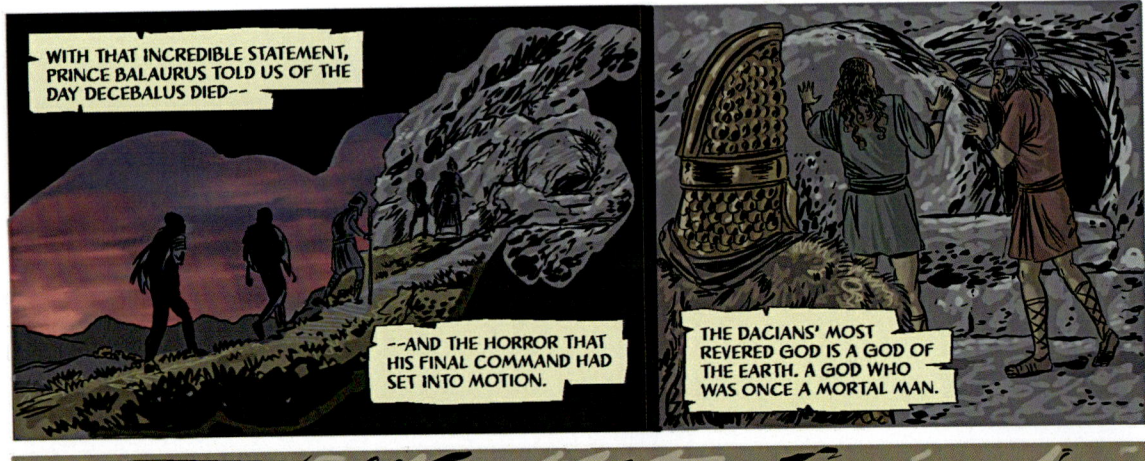

WITH THAT INCREDIBLE STATEMENT, PRINCE BALAURUS TOLD US OF THE DAY DECEBALUS DIED--

--AND THE HORROR THAT HIS FINAL COMMAND HAD SET INTO MOTION.

THE DACIANS' MOST REVERED GOD IS A GOD OF THE EARTH. A GOD WHO WAS ONCE A MORTAL MAN.

THIS MAN WAS A PHILOSOPHER, WITH A PROMISE OF ETERNAL LIFE AFTER DEATH FOR ALL WHO FOLLOWED HIS TEACHINGS.

HE BUILT A STONE CHAMBER OVER A RUMORED GATE TO THE UNDERWORLD, AND HAD HIS FOLLOWERS SEAL HIM IN. HE WOULD DESCEND, HE SAID, AND RETURN TO LIFE ONE YEAR LATER WITH THE SECRETS OF IMMORTALITY IN TOW.

A YEAR PASSED, AND HIS ACOLYTES OPENED THE TOMB--

--BUT THEIR MASTER WAS NO LONGER THE MAN THEY KNEW.

BY THE GRACE OF SOME HIGHER DEITY, ONE OF THEM MANAGED TO PIN THE CREATURE INTO HIS GRAVE BEFORE HE COULD ESCAPE INTO THE WORLD. THEY SEWED HIS MOUTH AND EYES SHUT WITH THONGS AND RE-SEALED THE CHAMBER.

THIS WAS NEARLY A THOUSAND YEARS AGO, AND HIS SECRET WAS CAREFULLY GUARDED BY HIS PRIESTS AND THE DACIAN KING.

UNTIL DECEBALUS ORDERED HE BE SET FREE.

ONLY THE PRINCE HAD ESCAPED. HE HAD SEALED THE TOMB BEHIND HIM AND PRAYED THAT IT WOULD REMAIN SO.

THE EVIDENCE OF HIS FAILURE WAS NOW ALL TOO CLEAR.

DECEBALUS'S MISGUIDED REVENGE AGAINST THE ROMANS WOULD HAVE THE GOD'S CHILDREN RUN UNCHECKED ACROSS THE WORLD, PLUNGING IT INTO ETERNAL DARKNESS.

HE DID NOT COUNT ON ONE OF HIS OWN REACHING OUT TO HIS HATED ENEMY--

--WITH THE WEAPONS THEY NEEDED TO DEFEAT THEM.

EEYAAAH!

WHAT'S... HAPPENING?

IT'S STARTING.

PLEASE--

NOT UNTIL YOU ARE DONE.

THE WEAPONS. A THOUSAND YEARS OF CAREFULLY-GUARDED DACIAN LORE ABOUT THE GOD'S TRUE NATURE.

THE STAKE OF WOOD THAT IMMOBILIZED HIM REINTRODUCED THEM TO PAIN. SO IT WOULD EVER CAUSE THEM PAIN, AND SO THEY WOULD EVER FEAR IT.

THE EVIL SPIRITS POSSESSING THE GOD ARE A VAST MULTITUDE, AND WERE NEARLY MINDLESS WHEN THEY TOOK HIM, KNOWING ONLY HUNGER FOR LIFE, FOR **BLOOD**, IN THEIR ETERNITY DOWN IN THE DARK.

ORDINARY WHITE ASH. IT COVERS THE PROVINCE, SO THE LEGIONS USE IT TO BUILD THEIR FORTRESS WALLS, AND TO CARVE THE WEAPONS THEY USE IN PRACTICE DRILLS.

THEY ALSO FEAR RUSHING WATER. IT IS AN UNPASSABLE BARRIER FOR DEAD THINGS, AND ITS PURIFYING FORCE STRIPS THE SPIRIT FROM ITS HOST UPON CONTACT.

FIRE IS ANOTHER PURIFIER, WITH NO FIRE SURER THAN THE SUN ITSELF. THIS IS WHY BALAURUS HAD BURNED HE COLONY.

THE BEARERS OF THE GOD'S PLAGUE-- THESE "NOSOPHOROI," AS ONE OF THE GREEK AUXILIARIES CALLED THEM--HIDE IN DENS IN THE EARTH DURING THE DAY. THE PRINCE SHOWED US HOW TO FIND THEM.

BUT THERE WERE THOUSANDS OF THESE CREATURES, AND WE WERE ONLY FINDING HANDFULS.
WORSE--THEY WERE CHANGING.
RRRAAGH!
THE ONCE-MINDLESS THINGS WHO HAD LEARNED PAIN WERE LEARNING OTHER THINGS. THEY BEGAN TO HIDE FROM US, TO TRICK US, TO ANTICIPATE OUR PLANS.
SOME WERE EVEN BECOMING THE PEOPLE WHOSE BODIES THEY HAD TAKEN.
FA... THER...
IT MADE THEM NO LESS MONSTROUS. NO LESS EVIL.
SERVING... THE EN-E-MY NOW... CLAU-DI-US? HOW FAR YOU HAVE FAL-LEN...
THIS ISN'T WORKING!
IT JUST KEEPS SPREADING. AT THIS RATE EVERYONE IN THE PROVINCE WILL BE DEAD BY AUTUMN!
WE NEED TO FIND THE GOD. TO DRAW HIM OUT.
AND HOW SHOULD WE GO ABOUT DOING THAT?
WE WERE ATTEMPTING TO DO THAT WHEN YOUR LEGIONS ATTACKED US.
WE WERE TRYING TO LOOK LIKE PREY, SO THEY WOULD ATTACK US ALL AT ONCE--
--AND YOU DREW US IN AS WELL.
WE'LL TRY AGAIN. BUT THIS TIME--
--WE USE EVERYONE.

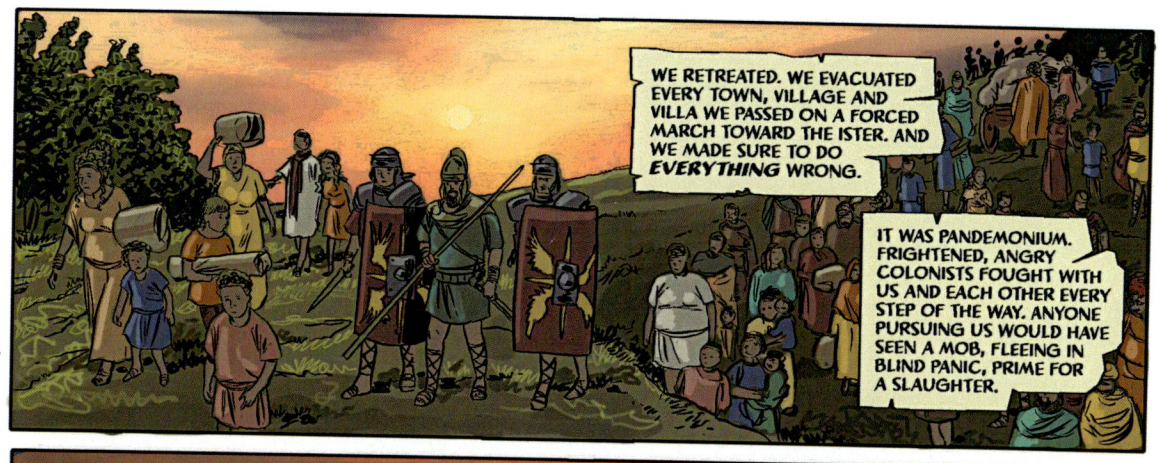

WE RETREATED. WE EVACUATED EVERY TOWN, VILLAGE AND VILLA WE PASSED ON A FORCED MARCH TOWARD THE ISTER. AND WE MADE SURE TO DO *EVERYTHING* WRONG.

IT WAS PANDEMONIUM. FRIGHTENED, ANGRY COLONISTS FOUGHT WITH US AND EACH OTHER EVERY STEP OF THE WAY. ANYONE PURSUING US WOULD HAVE SEEN A MOB, FLEEING IN BLIND PANIC, PRIME FOR A SLAUGHTER.

WE CAMPED IN A PLACE HEMMED IN ON THREE SIDES BY A RIVER. NON-COMBATANTS WERE PLACED IN THE REAR, WITH MEN READY TO SLIT THE THROATS OF EVERY MAN, WOMAN AND CHILD IF IT CAME TO IT.

THE REST OF US FORMED OUR LINES, CUT OUR PALMS, AND WAITED FOR THE FOG--THE SPECTRAL HERALD OF THE GOD--TO ARRIVE.

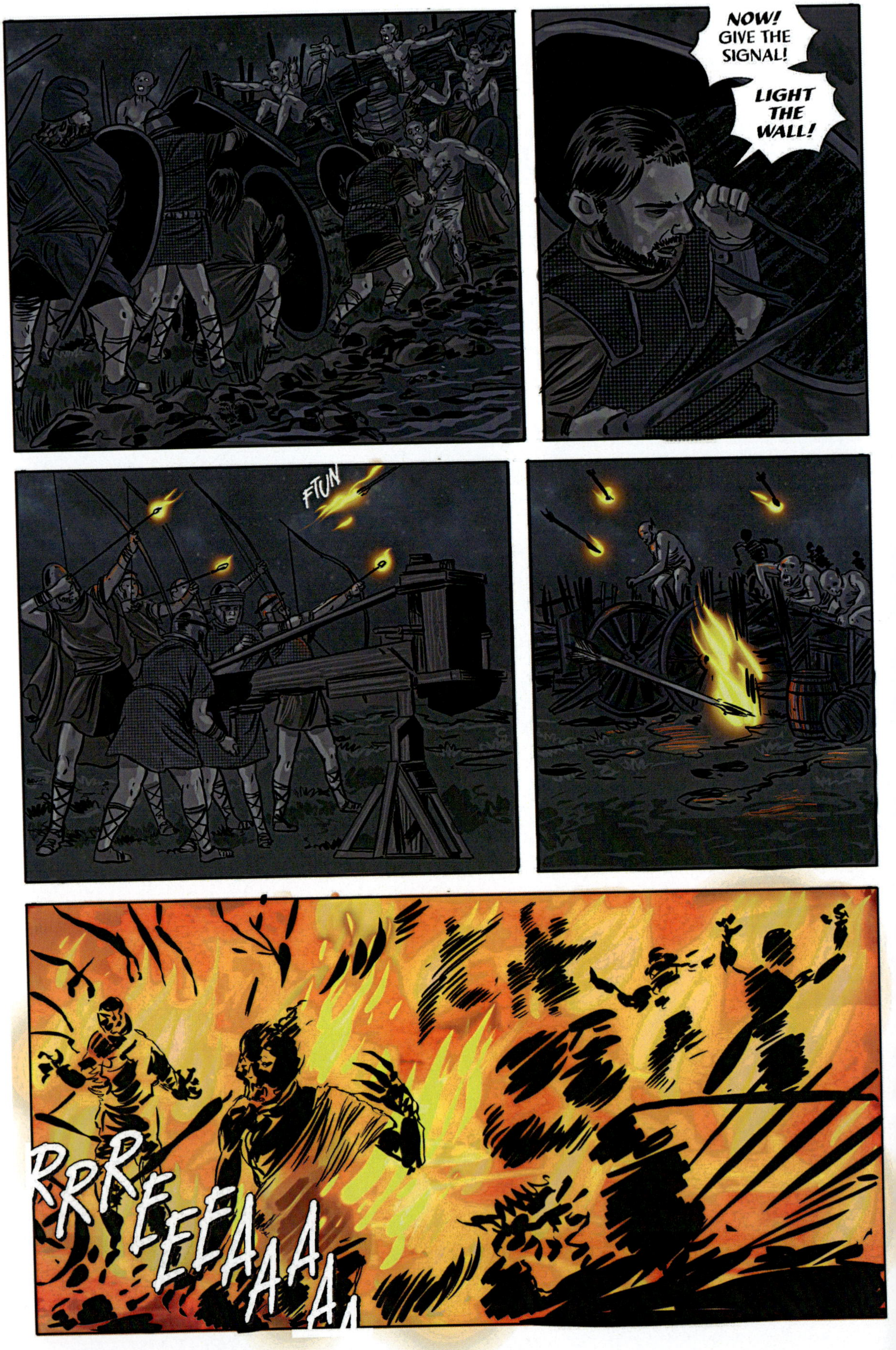
NOW! GIVE THE SIGNAL!
LIGHT THE WALL!
FTUN
RRRREEEAAAAA

PUUUSH!

The trap was sprung. This time, it was the creatures who were the panicked prey.

It was still a close-run thing. We died by the dozens. They died by more.

It was a fight we could win. That we were GOING to win.

Or so I thought, before I saw...

GODS ABOVE--

I SAW THE GOD HIMSELF, GIGANTIC, TERRIBLE TO BEHOLD.

BALAURUS WAS BATTLING HIM. I DON'T KNOW HOW HE WITHSTOOD THE GOD'S FURY.

I COULD ONLY STAND, HELPLESS, WAITING TO SEE WHICH MONSTER WOULD WIN OUT.

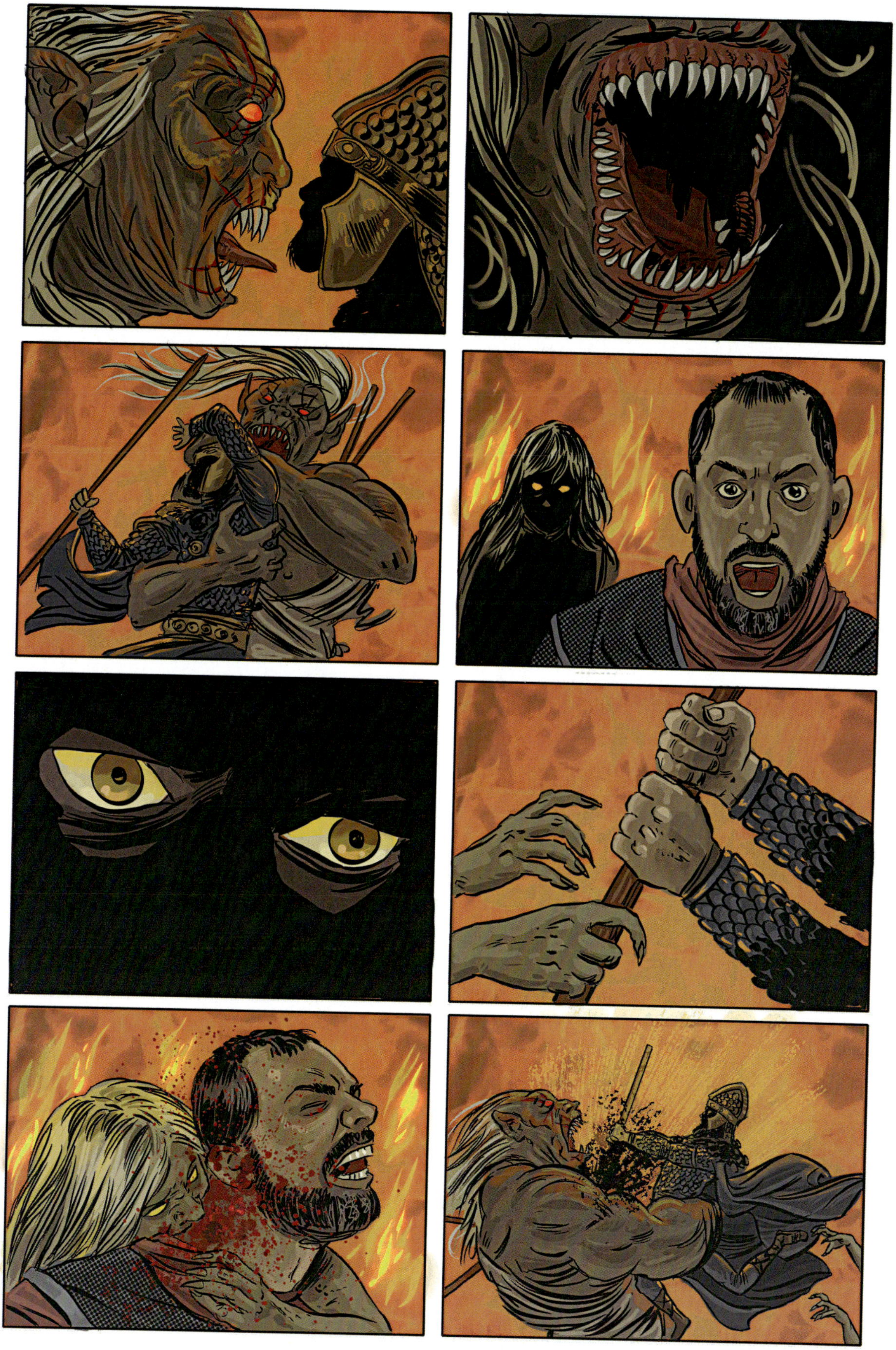

ULTIMATELY, IT WAS NEITHER.

BALAURUS SUCCEEDED IN DESTROYING THE GOD, CAESAR. BUT HE DID NOT SURVIVE THE NIGHT.

AND I REGRET TO REPORT--

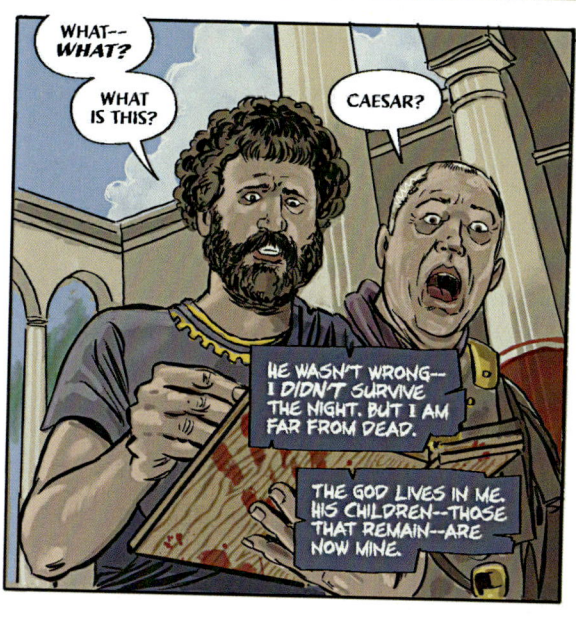

--NEITHER DID I.

SHNK

I HOPE I HAVE YOUR ATTENTION NOW, HADRIAN.

THIS ISN'T THAT POMPOUS PRIG CLAUDIUS ANYMORE, BY THE WAY.

WHAT-- WHAT?

WHAT IS THIS?

CAESAR?

HE WASN'T WRONG-- I DIDN'T SURVIVE THE NIGHT. BUT I AM FAR FROM DEAD.

THE GOD LIVES IN ME. HIS CHILDREN--THOSE THAT REMAIN--ARE NOW MINE.

UNLIKE HIM, I AM BETTER ABLE TO CONTROL MY APPETITES.

THE QUESTION IS...CAN YOU CONTROL YOURS?

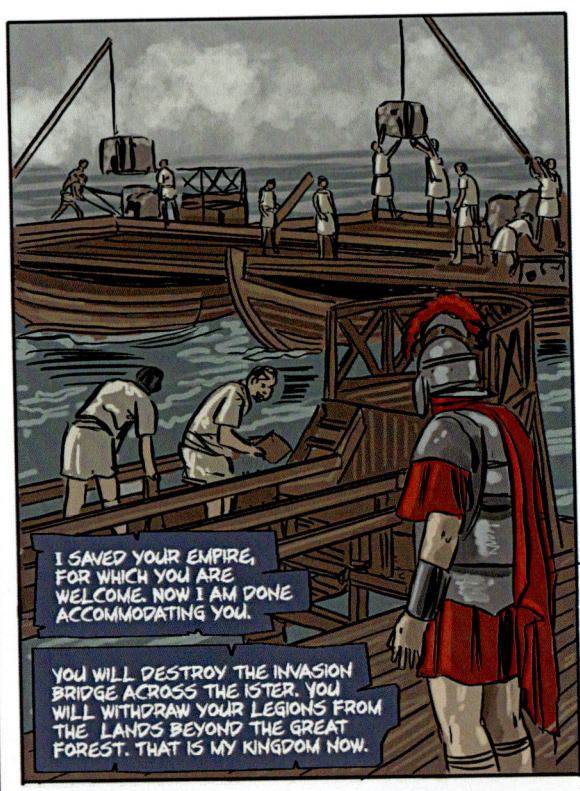

MALE PARTA MALE DILABVNTVR

I SAVED YOUR EMPIRE, FOR WHICH YOU ARE WELCOME. NOW I AM DONE ACCOMMODATING YOU.

YOU WILL DESTROY THE INVASION BRIDGE ACROSS THE ISTER. YOU WILL WITHDRAW YOUR LEGIONS FROM THE LANDS BEYOND THE GREAT FOREST. THAT IS MY KINGDOM NOW.

EXPAND YOUR REALM NO FURTHER. KEEP TO YOUR DACIA, AND I WILL KEEP TO MINE.

OTHERWISE I WILL SHOW YOU WHAT A WORLD OF DARKNESS TRULY IS.

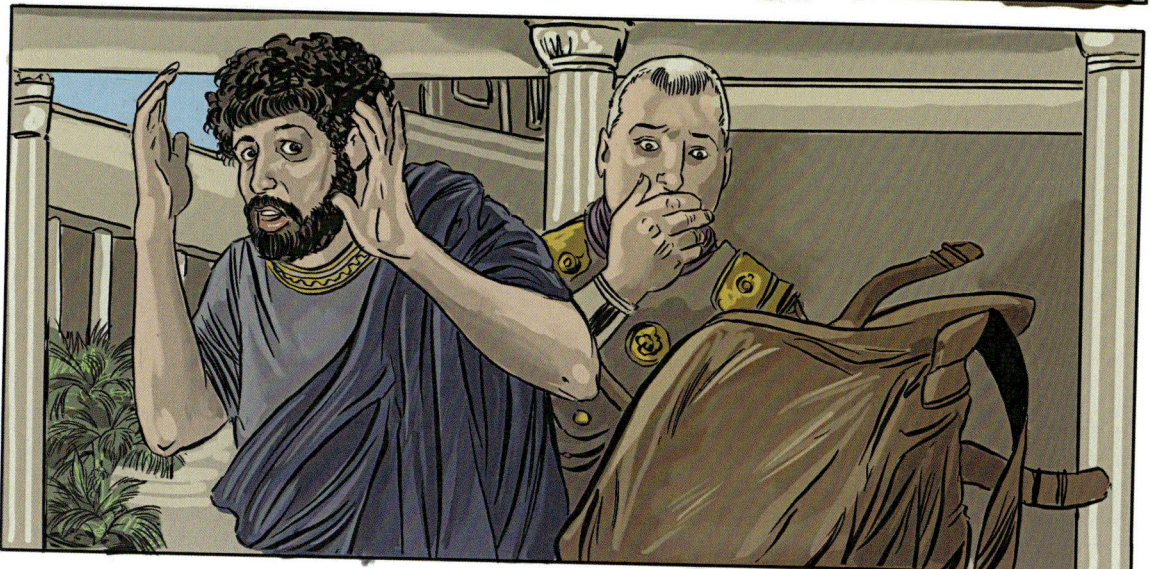

ENJOY YOUR STAY IN MY BEAUTIFUL LAND, FOR AS LONG AS IT LASTS.

AMICUM TUUM, B.

FINIS